THE MYSTERY OF
MICROSNEEZIA

Other titles in this series:
The Mystery of the Backlot Banshee

Learning Company Books
A division of Riverdeep, Inc.
500 Redwood Boulevard, Novato, CA 94947, USA

Editor: Brenda Kienan
Illustrations: Animotion, Inc.
Cover design: Mez Design
Page layout: Creative Media Applications

ISBN 0-7630-7619-8

First printing: March 2004
Printed in the United States of America

10 9 8 7 6 5 4 3 2 1

Visit Learning Company Books at
www.learningcompanybooks.com.

The publisher thanks Kenny Dinkin
for his creative contributions.

THE MYSTERY OF
MICROSNEEZIA

Ellen Weiss and Mel Friedman

Learning Company Books
A division of Riverdeep, Inc.

PROLOGUE

The jungle was as dense as any on earth. Enormous trees, covered with vines, swayed above the thick green undergrowth. Strange chirps, buzzes, howls, and screeches rang out overhead.

Through the steamy rainforest trudged a brown-bearded man: Dr. Horace Pythagoras, world-famous scientist. He was accompanied by a small band of hardy guides.

Dr. Pythagoras raised his machete to hack at a vine that blocked his path. A gigantic mosquito dive-bombed him. He stopped, waved his arms, and exclaimed, "Blast this island! Gnats the size of baseballs, mosquitoes as big as pigeons, and there's not one plant that doesn't cause sneezing or wheezing or itching or fainting. It's no wonder nobody ever comes here."

"We don't like it much ourselves," said Freddy, his head guide. "We wouldn't live here if a whole ship full of our great-grandparents hadn't been marooned. No airlines or shipping companies have stopped here in three years." He blew his nose loudly.

One of the other guides scratched at a huge mosquito bite. "You don't have it so bad, Dr.

Pythagoras," he said. "The bugs buzz right around your head, but they never bite you. You're lucky."

"This would be a beautiful place," said Dr. Pythagoras, "If only—" He stopped in mid-sentence, and his eyes lit up. "Just a moment!" he said. "That pink root... those blue spots... that can only be... The vegemecium! The largest single-celled vegetable on earth! At last, I have found it!"

Freddy bent down to inspect the plant. "Gee, it looks like a big rutabaga to me," he said.

Dr. Pythagoras took out a pocketknife and a plastic bag. "I can't wait to get a look at this thing under a microscope," he said, shaving off a bit of the pink root and dropping it into the bag. "This could be a great discovery."

The guides were backing away. "Don't you know this thing is bad luck?" said one of them. "Don't touch it!"

"Baah," said Dr. Pythagoras. "Pure superstition. I am a man of science, and there is no place in science for... *Aaaahhhh!*"

A huge vine snaked out from nowhere and grabbed Dr. Pythagoras by the ankle, snatching him upward until he was dangling upside-down in the air.

HAPPY BIRTHDAY, JONI?

The fog was rolling in over the San Francisco hills.
At Joni Savage's house, the ClueFinders—the
world's foremost team of kid detectives—were
involved in a high-level meeting.

"Pepperoni, for sure," said Santiago.

"No way, dude, we gotta have mushrooms," said
Owen. His black hair caught the light as he shook
his head.

"I just wish they made bubble gum-flavored
pizza," said Leslie wistfully.

"You and your bubble gum," said Santiago.
"Who would think somebody so smart would be so
in love with bubble gum?"

Leslie Clark, the brainiest and best-read of all
the ClueFinders, had recently developed a
surprising passion for pink bubble gum.

"We all have our idiosyncrasies," said Leslie.

"Which are…?" Owen asked.

"Quirks," she replied. "And I know they don't
make bubble gum pizza. So I vote for broccoli."

"*Broccoli?* Broccoli's the pits!"

"Pep-per-o-ni! Pep-per-o-ni!" Santiago chanted.

A loud whistle silenced the din. It was Joni. "Okay, listen up you guys!" she said. "It's my birthday, so I say what kind of pizza we order."

Everyone looked a little sheepish. "You're totally right, Joni," said Owen. "Our bad. It's your birthday. What kind of pizza do you want?"

"Hmmm," said Joni. "Let me think." She twirled the end of one of her thick red braids, considering.

"Okay," she said. "What we're getting is a large broccoli pizza—"

"Awwww," said Owen and Santiago together.

"—with pepperoni and mushrooms," she continued. "And sausage for me."

"Yaayyy!" said Leslie.

"You *rule!*" Owen yelled.

"A born leader," Santiago agreed.

Owen reached for the phone. "I'll order it."

"Do it quick, okay?" said Joni. "I'm waiting for my birthday call from Uncle Horace. I don't want him to have trouble getting through. He's away on some scientific expedition, as usual. Right now, he's in Microsneezia."

"Microsneezia?" asked Owen.

"Yup. Nobody ever goes there; I hardly know

anything about it. He's looking for some kind of big plant. Anyway, it might be hard for him to call, and I don't want him to get a busy signal."

"Okay, I'll order in a flash," said Owen, punching in the pizzeria's number in seconds using all the fingers of his right hand.

"You know the number by heart?" said Santiago.

"Pizza is my life, dude," said Owen.

"So," said Leslie. "While we're waiting for the pizza, this might be a good time to bestow the—"

"Presents!" whooped Owen. "Cool!"

They all sat down around the coffee table. "Let the unwrapping begin," said Owen. "Here's mine."

He handed Joni a package wrapped haphazardly in Christmas paper, even though it was July. Joni hefted it in her hand. "Feels like a book," she said.

"Rats, you guessed it," he said.

She tore open the paper. "*Everything You Need to Know About Skateboarding,*" she read. "Hmmm. Thanks, Owen. I'll start reading it the second I get a skateboard."

Joni didn't mind getting a skateboard book from him. Owen Lam's infectious enthusiasm for anything athletic—especially his skateboard—was part of what made him loveable.

"Ready for my present?" said a voice. It was LapTrap, their trusty computer, hovering overhead.

"LapTrap, you got me a present?" said Joni. "You shouldn't have." She waited expectantly for it.

"Oh," said LapTrap, "you can't see it. It's a little program I made up. A special math-assistance program designed just for Joni Savage."

"LapTrap, I can't believe you did that!" said Joni.

Next, Santiago passed Joni a small package, beautifully wrapped. "I hope you like this," he told her. She could see the care in his dark eyes.

She opened the gift carefully. Inside was a small black box with a series of colored lights that traveled along the edges, blinking in sequence. Clearly, this was a classic creation by Santiago Rivera, ace inventor of gadgets and gizmos.

"Wow," said Joni. "What is it?"

"It's a reticulating transponder," Santiago replied. "Just for you."

"Great!" said Joni. She furrowed her brow. "Er... what's it for?"

"Use it any time you need a reticulating transponder, of course," he said. "It'll come in handy in dozens of ways."

"I bet it will," she said, trying not to look too

befuddled by it. "Thanks, Santiago."

Finally, Leslie staggered over to the table and dropped an enormous package onto the coffee table in front of Joni. It landed with a *wham.*

"Oh, wow," said Joni. She pulled back the flowered paper, revealing a very old dictionary.

"*Webster's Unabridged,* 1913," Leslie said. "I knew I had to buy it for you."

"I'm—I'm speechless."

"Well, you won't be ever again with this dictionary," said Leslie, so excited that her dark curls shook as she spoke.

Suddenly, the red videophone started making urgent noises. The videophone was used by the ClueFinders for important communications. "What on earth could *that* be?" wondered Owen. "We're all here, so why should it be ringing?"

Joni leaped to her feet. "It's gotta be Uncle Horace!" she cried. "He must have figured out some way to get a message through to it."

They all stood around the videophone, squinting at the screen. The words "Sunrise 441" appeared. Below this was a message of some sort. "The message is encrypted," said Santiago, "but I don't know the code."

"'Sunrise 441' is a distress message I invented with Uncle Horace when I was little!" said Joni. "He must be in real trouble to use it!" She stared at the symbols on the screen. "This is a code we worked out. We haven't used it in so long, I can't remember where I put the key to it."

She rummaged frantically in the drawers of a big roll-top desk in the corner. "Oh, I wish my grandma had some kind of a filing system," she wailed, flinging papers this way and that.

Joni was living, as she sometimes did, with her grandmother. Joni's parents were political science professors and had to spend a lot of time overseas. Santiago was also living at Joni's grandma's. His parents, a pair of Latin American revolutionaries, had put him in the care of Joni's family, who were their close friends. The arrangement worked well for everyone. It enabled Joni and Santiago to keep going to school without being uprooted. Joni's grandmother enjoyed having kids around the house. Plus, she had the coolest old Victorian house in San Francisco.

"Aha!" Joni yelled, yanking a sheet of paper from the bottom drawer. "Here it is!" She ran back to the videophone. "Let's see," she said, studying the code.

Use the code below to translate
Uncle Horace's message.

A=⊀,B=✦,C=ᵘᵢ,D=➐,E=Ⅵ,F=⊄,G=⊔,H=Ξ
I=1,J=⊅,K=⊐,L=⌐,M=∠,N=ᴧ,O=△,P=◁,Q=⊏
R=➐,S=�‾,T=↓,U=◻,V=Y,W=□,X=Δ,Y=∨,Z=◁

CHAPTER 2

BUMPY LANDING

"Let's go, ClueFinders!" cried Joni. "Uncle Horace needs help! We have to go to Microsneezia to rescue him! We'd better leave right away and—hey, where the heck is Microsneezia, anyway?"

"Microsneezia," said Leslie without missing a beat, "is a group of infinitesimal islands in the South Pacific. The Microsneezian Islands are largely unexplored, due to their extremely inhospitable environment. They are riddled with noxious plants and incredibly irritating insects. Captain Cook gave the islands one sniff and decided to keep going."

"Oh, wow," said Owen. "It's a good thing we have a walking encyclopedia around here."

Meanwhile, LapTrap was in a dither. "Oh, great," he said. "Here we go again. Let's just run off to some miserable, horrible corner of the world and look for as much trouble as possible."

"LapTrap," said Joni. "How can you even think of not rescuing Uncle Horace? He's the one who saved you from having to work for the military, remember?"

"That's true," said LapTrap sheepishly. "He did save me." LapTrap had been developed by the military. He was dubbed a T.U.R.T.L.E., which stood for Turbo-charged Ultra Rugged Terrain Laptop Equipment. But he had proved not to be ultra-rugged at all. He had whined and complained and chickened out so constantly that the army had finally given up and handed him over to Uncle Horace to use in his work.

"And then Uncle Horace gave you to us, to help us in *our* work," Joni said. "Aren't you glad you get to hang around with us?"

"Usually," said LapTrap.

"Well, then quit complaining and help us figure out how we get to Microsneezia," Joni said.

"All right, all right," said LapTrap. "He's given us his position—33 degrees south latitude, 97 degrees west longitude. That should tell us which of the islands he was on when he called." He did some quick calculations. "I've got it," LapTrap said. "It's the largest one: Inner Microsneezia."

"Let's go!" said Owen.

"I'll figure out what we need to bring," said Santiago.

"And I'll start making travel arrangements," said

Joni. "Microsneezia, here we come!"

"Is this the best you could do?" said LapTrap, looking down queasily as the ground rushed away below them.

"Yes, it's the best I could do," said Joni, "and we're lucky to get it. Nobody comes here. That's why we had to travel 48 hours by biplane, six hours over land by donkey, and then rent this hot-air balloon to take us the rest of the way."

"Yeah," laughed Owen. "Lewey Leakey's Balloon and Costume Rentals. Inspires a lot of confidence."

Joni looked up at their bright blue-and-yellow balloon. "I think it's great," she said. "Give it a little more gas, Santiago."

Santiago turned the flame up a bit, and the balloon lifted higher into the air. "This balloon is actually perfect," Joni said. "Since there are no ports in Microsneezia, and no airfields, this gives us the best way in."

After a little while, Santiago turned the burner off and they drifted along in silence. They were borne on air currents, so there wasn't even any sound from the wind.

"It's so quiet," said Santiago, putting on a set of earphones, "I can home in on Uncle Horace's heartbeat." He began twiddling the dials on his newest invention, a super-sensitive listening device that could pick up a heartbeat from miles away.

"Anything yet?" Leslie asked.

"Not so far," he said. "Only lots of insects."

"How will you be able to tell Uncle Horace's heartbeat from somebody else's?" Joni asked.

"Well, when I first invented this machine, your uncle was interested in it," he said. "He let me try it out on him, so now I have his heartbeat in the machine's memory."

LapTrap was still looking down from the balloon's gondola. "I can't see how we're going to be able to land," he said. "There's nothing down there but trees, trees, trees. And mountains. We're probably doomed."

"We'll figure something out," said Joni. "That's why we're the ClueFinders."

They skimmed along above the lush rainforest. Owen, balancing surfboard-style on the lip of the balloon's gondola, began to sniff the air. "It's no wonder nobody comes here," he said. "This place stinks. I can smell it all the way up here."

"Eew, you're right," Joni agreed.

"Hang on, I'm getting something," said Santiago. "It's really faint, but it's something."

"Everybody be quiet so he can hear," said Joni.

There was utter silence in the gondola as Santiago concentrated. But—what was that gray, cloudlike thing zigzagging upward towards them from the jungle? It buzzed and hummed as it traveled closer.

"What the heck is that?" Joni said.

Owen climbed down into the gondola and dug his field glasses out of his backpack. He adjusted the focus. "Cute," he said. "Looks like ladybugs."

Leslie frowned. "Here, let me see," she said, taking the binoculars. "There is no species of ladybug indigenous to Microsneezia. Hmm. Maybe they're locusts."

The swarm of bugs zoomed right past the kids, ignoring the gondola and snaking upward—toward the balloon itself.

"The balloon! Dudes—they want the balloon!" cried Owen.

The bugs began attacking the balloon. They bit furiously, splitting into teams to chew holes all over the balloon's surface. Slowly, it deflated.

"Okay, gang, it's time for Plan B," said Joni, reaching into a large canvas bag and pulling out parasails for everyone. "We'd better get out of this balloon, fast." Then she strapped on her parasail.

"Awesome!" exclaimed Owen.

"I can't believe I'm doing this," said Santiago. He stuffed the heartbeat detector into his knapsack, just in case, and shakily strapped on his parasail.

"Hold my hand," Joni said. "We'll jump together." Santiago closed his eyes, grabbed Joni's hand, and over they went.

"You too, LapTrap," Joni called up to him.

"I don't want to!" he called. "Do I have to?"

"YES, you have to!" she called, her voice getting fainter as she dropped farther away.

Grumbling, LapTrap went over the side.

Waiting her turn, Leslie applied some last-minute strawberry lip balm and prepared to jump. "This is my good-luck lip balm," she said to Owen. Then, her parasail firmly in place, she jumped, leaving Owen to jump last.

But no sooner had Leslie begun her descent than the swarm of bugs attacked her parasail. In seconds, they had eaten a large hole in it. She plummeted helplessly earthward. "ClueFinders!"

she shrieked. "Heeeelllp!"

"Have no fear, Owen is here!" came a yell from above. Owen leaped into thin air without pulling the cord to open his parasail. Arms at his sides, pointing his body like a rocket, he bulleted toward Leslie, scooped her up, and then pulled his cord. His sail opened above them like a big bright flower, and Leslie let go of her sail. It fell to the ground, bedraggled and useless. Leslie held Owen tightly as they drifted down.

"I don't like to fly this hi-i-i-i-gh!" wailed LapTrap as he buzzed past Joni and the others.

"You'll be fine," Joni called to him. "I happen to know that you're rated for 16,000 feet."

"Whooee!" Owen yelled as they all glided over the forest. "Dudes, this is way awesome!"

But they still had to somehow get through the thick cover of trees to land. There was nothing to do but take a deep breath and crash through the green canopy.

It was a messy affair. By the time the ClueFinders reached the ground, they were all bumped, bruised, scratched, and scraped. The group removed their parasail harnesses and sat on the ground for a while, panting.

"Something tells me we have company," said Owen, scratching at a bite he'd just gotten.

"Look out!" said Joni. "Giant bug at two o'clock!"

Owen looked up just in time to see a pigeon-sized mosquito heading straight for his right arm. Its long stinger was the size of a knitting needle. "*Bzzzzzz!*" it went loudly. Owen windmilled his arms at the huge mosquito, and it buzzed off to find another victim. All the ClueFinders started waving their arms frantically. Finally the bug moved along.

"Can we go home now?" whined LapTrap.

The group stood up and began looking for a trail. But the jungle was dense on every side. "We'll just have to whack our way through," said Joni, pulling a machete from her backpack.

Santiago stopped walking for a moment so he could listen to his monitor. "I'm still getting a faint heartbeat," he said. "It's to our left."

So they set off to the left, Joni in the lead, with Santiago right behind her. She cut and slashed away with the machete, but it was slow going. It was impossible not to get bitten by an assortment of horrible buzzing things: gigantic mosquitoes, green flies, things that looked like flying cockroaches. In minutes, they were all madly scratching at the same kind of enormous bites that Uncle Horace's guides had endured—all except Leslie.

"Hey, how come you didn't get bitten?" Owen asked her as he slapped at a huge gnat.

"Perhaps I have some natural immunity to entomological toxins," she speculated.

"I guess," said Owen.

"Hey, look at this," Joni said. "C'mere, everybody!"

They all clustered around her. "It's a trail," she said. "And it's been cut recently. I think we've found the path that was blazed by Uncle Horace!" They could see where vines and tree branches had been hacked through with a machete. "Let's follow it, ClueFinders!" Joni said.

The group made their way behind her down the path, which was sometimes so faint that they could only find it by spotting a broken leaf or a snapped twig. Periodically, they stopped to wipe the sweat out of their eyes and scratch their bites. "I hate it when my glasses fog up," Joni said, wiping her round spectacles.

Finally, after another hour of walking, Joni gave

a shout back to the others. "I think we've found what Uncle Horace was looking for!" she yelled.

Ahead of them, in a little clearing, was a gigantic plant. Huge pink air-roots with blue spots waved gently in the air all around it.

"This is it!" she exclaimed. "The vegemecium!"

"Looks like a giant rutabaga," said Owen, inspecting it.

Behind them, Leslie let out a gasp. "Guys! Help!" she called.

They ran to the edge of the clearing. There they saw what had made Leslie gasp. A man, dangling upside-down from a vine, was squirming uncomfortably. Beside him was another hanging vine; dangling from that one was a lone boot.

"I'd know that boot anywhere!" said Joni. "It's Uncle Horace's!"

Quickly, the team worked to cut the man free. They lowered him gently to the ground. "Uhhh," he groaned, rubbing his ankle. "That smarts."

"Are you okay?" "Who are you?" "Where's Uncle Horace?" "What happened?" they all asked.

"I was his head guide on this trip," said the man. "My name is Freddy. Dr. Pythagoras got snatched up by the giant plant, and we all got scared and ran away, but then I felt guilty so I returned. When I got back, he was gone, all except for his shoe. And then I was snatched up."

"Look, guys, over here," said Owen from a short distance away. "Here's his videophone."

Sure enough, Uncle Horace's videophone was lying on the ground. It was in sad shape, but a dim, garbled message could be read on its screen.

"Maybe it's a last message he left for us to find," said Joni.

"Can you read it?" Owen asked her.

She squinted at it. "I can't figure it out," she said. "The letters are all broken, and I think they got scrambled, too. LapTrap, can you enhance the image so the letters are clearer?"

DAHE
TROHN YB
SHNERTOAT

LapTrap plugged the videophone into one of his ports and went to work on it. Soon he had made a lot of progress, and the letters were much clearer.

"Thanks, LapTrap," said Joni. "Now we have to see if we can unscramble it so it spells something."

Unscramble the letters to decode this secret message.

CHAPTER 3

S.N.A.I.L.L.'S PACE

The ClueFinders team made their arduous way through the jungle, keeping their heading at north-by-northeast. Freddy, Uncle Horace's guide, had taken his leave of them, knowing his family would be frantic for news of him.

The ClueFinders were all exhausted, and the bugs were still a constant nuisance. The team slogged along, tripped by vines and scratched by branches.

"Ow!" said Leslie. "I just twisted my ankle."

"Can you walk?" Joni asked.

"I'm okay," said Leslie. But she was limping.

"Here, let me carry your backpack," said Joni. She took Leslie's pack, which was fairly heavy, and shouldered it along with her own.

"Thanks," said Leslie. "You're the best."

"What are detective teammates for?" said Joni.

They fell into silence, concentrating on putting one foot in front of the other. Even LapTrap forged ahead without complaining.

"Hey," Joni said suddenly after a while,

"I haven't been bitten by anything for fifteen whole minutes. Hooray!"

"Shhh!" said Santiago. "You'll jinx it."

Gradually, the light began to fade. They would have to camp in the jungle. They were bummed that they hadn't found Uncle Horace yet, but there was no sense in going on in the dark.

The ClueFinders carved a clearing to sleep in, unhooked their sleeping bags from their packs, and spread out their gear. They were glad to take off their packs. Each one contained a large water bottle, water-purifying pills, some food, a change of clothes, a compass, a first-aid kit, sunscreen, and various other items.

"Leslie, can I keep your backpack to use for a pillow?" Joni asked.

"Sure," said Leslie. "I won't need it. I don't sleep with a pillow."

They all stretched out and tried to get comfortable.

"Hmmm," said Joni in the dark. "What's that unmistakable scent coming out of your backpack, Leslie? Tell me you didn't bring bubble gum halfway around the world."

"Well, just a six-dozen-pack," said Leslie.

"I guess it opened up when you rolled on it."

"Leslie, you gum-chewing maniac!" said Owen.

"I brought some along in case I got a craving," said Leslie. "You never know."

"Leslie, you're full of surprises," said Owen, laughing.

"Never mind, you guys," said Joni. "We better get some sleep so we can get started early."

They all agreed, and after half an hour of tossing, turning, and batting at bugs, they were fast asleep.

In the morning, they awoke hungry, achy, and miserable. They had all slept terribly, and been tormented by bugs all night. Nobody was in a good mood—except Joni, who had been mercifully—and mysteriously—ignored by the bugs.

"LapTrap," said Joni, "why don't you go scout out some firewood so we can cook breakfast?"

"Oh, sure," he grumbled to himself as he moved off. "Make the computer do it. The computer doesn't even eat breakfast."

"I heard that," said Joni.

◧◩

LapTrap hovered over the forest floor, looking for dead wood and continuing to grumble. "Sure. LapTrap will look for firewood," he muttered. "Whatever it is, LapTrap will take care of it."

He flew down to look at a piece of a branch that was wedged in at the base of a large rock. No good for firewood, though: the branch was rotten. When he rose above the rock again, LapTrap found himself looking into his own face.

This was surprising. Why would there be a mirror right in the middle of the jungle? And why did the image look so real?

LapTrap cautiously moved right. The other LapTrap moved right.

LapTrap ducked to the left. The other LapTrap ducked to the left.

LapTrap wiggled his front end. The other LapTrap wiggled his front end.

LapTrap raised an eyebrow. The other LapTrap raised an eyebrow.

LapTrap sneezed.

"Gesundheit," said the other LapTrap.

Hmm, thought LapTrap. This was no mirror.

But LapTrap had not figured it out quite fast enough. Now he was in deep trouble. The other LapTrap beamed a dazzling blue ray of light straight at him. *BZZZZT!*

LapTrap plummeted to the ground like a rock, half the circuits on his motherboard fried.

"Wh-who *are* you?" he managed to say in a crackly voice to his double, who was now hovering triumphantly over him.

"Meet your worst nightmare, T.U.R.T.L.E.," said LapTrap's attacker. "S.N.A.I.L.L.'s the name."

"S.N.A.I.L.L.?"

"Yes sirree. Superior Numerical Artificial Intelligence Logic Laptop. The military made me after they made you, only they got rid of that wimp chip of yours. They put a new and improved one into me—the devil chip. I'm meaner than a snake, and I like it that way."

"What are you doing here?" LapTrap asked him weakly.

"The army banished me to this island. I was too mean for even them to handle. They were going to destroy me, but Dr. Horace Pythagoras recommended that they send me to some miserable, forgotten corner of the earth instead.

Better I should have been sent to the crusher. I'm so *bored,* I could explode. And then, who should turn up here but Dr. Pythagoras himself, my tormentor. And now I have his little friends, the ClueFinders." He laughed a small, nasty laugh. "You might say I have a chip on my shoulder—a bad chip."

LapTrap could only give a weak, fizzling sound before his circuits went into a dead faint.

Joni was getting things ready for breakfast when LapTrap appeared—or so she thought. "Oh, there you are!" she said. "I thought you'd been kidnapped by pirates or something. Did you find firewood?"

"Yup, I found a really good stash," S.N.A.I.L.L. replied, using a voice like LapTrap's. "I also figured out how to get to Uncle Horace."

"Amazing!" said Joni. "That's great!" Then she looked again at the computer. "Three whole sentences without a complaint or whining. Do you feel okay?" She laid the back of her hand on his bright yellow brow.

The false LapTrap suddenly seemed to remember himself. "Oh, well, of course I'm not *happy* I had to go look for firewood. Don't get me wrong."

"That sounds more like you, LapTrap," said Joni with a laugh. "Don't suddenly go changing on us."

"Me? Never," said S.N.A.I.L.L., suppressing a snicker.

When breakfast was over, the team rolled up their sleeping bags and repacked their knapsacks. "I can carry mine today," Leslie told Joni. "A night's sleep did me a lot of good."

"I feel pretty good, too," said Joni, stretching. "Not one bite all night. Whoo-hoo!"

"Wish I could say the same," groaned Leslie. "I was bitten like mad last night."

"Now," Joni told the group, "LapTrap says he's figured out which way we have to go to find Uncle Horace." She turned to S.N.A.I.L.L. "Lead on, LapTrap," she said.

"All right, all right," he whined, remembering to sound like LapTrap.

They plunged into the jungle, slapping at bugs all the way. "Yikes!" called Joni. "I guess it's my turn to get bitten again. I don't like this!"

On they slogged, as the sun climbed higher and the jungle got steamier and steamier. It was impossible to walk more than a few feet without hacking away vines and leaves.

"Are you sure this is the way, LapTrap?" Joni asked, stopping to scratch her neck.

"Positive," said S.N.A.I.L.L., flying along just ahead of the group. "I—er—just figured it out this morning using my GPS tracking capability."

Before Joni could protest, he had led them to the edge of a steep ravine. They were all in danger of losing their footing and hurtling hundreds of feet to the bottom. Small stones and roots shifted under their feet, making every step treacherous as they then made their way down an impossibly narrow switchback. At one point, Leslie did slip, crashing into Joni ahead of her and sending them both into the beginning of a terrifying fall, until Joni managed to grab onto a tree trunk.

"You guys, let's tie ourselves together so we don't lose anybody," said Joni.

"Great idea!" said Leslie. "Maybe we can use one of those vines that wrap around the trees."

"Whoa, dudes—I'll get us a long one," said Owen. He scrambled up the slope to a tree with a long, sturdy vine, and cut it off with his pocket knife.

When he returned with the vine, they looped it

around themselves, one by one. "I know a good knot for this job," said Santiago. "My *papi* taught it to me when I was little. It'll hold like iron."

He tied each of his teammates to the line. "Remind me to thank your dad someday," Joni said.

They kept walking, still nervous but feeling more secure.

"This reminds me of the time we had to go down that giant slide in the toy store where we all got shrunk," said Owen. "Only that was way more fun. Remember, LapTrap?"

"What?" said S.N.A.I.L.L. "Slide? Oh, uh, sure. Sure I do."

The climb up the opposite side of the ravine was punishing. They finally hauled themselves over the edge, one by one, gasping for breath.

"LapTrap, was that really the only place we could cross?" asked Santiago.

"Yeah, that really was bad, dude," said Owen.

"According to my calculations, it was the best place to get through," said S.N.A.I.L.L. with false innocence. "Now, we'd better keep moving or we won't make it there before it gets dark."

They dragged themselves to their feet and kept walking.

"When are we going to get there?" moaned Owen after another hour or so.

"Not for a while," said S.N.A.I.L.L. "Keep up the pace."

Santiago was stopping more and more frequently to scratch his shin. Finally he took a good look at it. "Oh, brother," he said. "This isn't a bite. This looks like poison ivy. Or poison something."

The rest of them paused to look at the places that had been itching them. "Yep," said Joni. "I've got it, too. Only it's not poison ivy—it's something that only lives on this island."

"Sheesh—I'm allergic to something here, too," said Owen, rubbing his watery eyes. "I've never been allergic in my life, but now I'm buggin'."

"Me, too," agreed Joni and Santiago together. They both sneezed.

"Amazing," said Leslie. "I don't seem to have anything itchy or sneezy at all."

"Let's keep going," said S.N.A.I.L.L.

"Okay, okay," said Leslie. "Since when did you get so intrepid and indefatigable, anyway?"

"Inde-what?" asked Owen.

"Not being a chicken. And not getting tired,"

Joni translated.

"I knew that," Owen said.

They kept walking, the jungle buzzing all around them as they followed the impostor.

"What next, I wonder?" said Santiago. "This place is worse than that living island we went to with your grandfather, Leslie."

"Yes, maybe LapTrap can find some cryptiles to get us out of here," added Leslie, referring to the mysterious yellow bricks that had saved them.

"Think you can find us some, LapTrap?" Owen joked.

"I-I can try," said S.N.A.I.L.L. uncertainly. "What did they look like, again?"

Each of the ClueFinders silently thought the same thing: *How could LapTrap forget what cryptiles look like?* It was weird. LapTrap had a perfect memory, and the cryptiles had been important.

Suddenly, Joni let out a scream. "Quicksand!" she yelled. "I'm sinking! Don't follow me!"

Sure enough, she was slowly moving downward. The ground was a thick brown soup that sucked at whatever fell into it. Joni was in it up to her knees, and then, in no time, up to her waist.

"Don't struggle!" cried Leslie. "The more you

struggle, the more you'll submerge. Just try to make yourself flat and don't make any sudden movements." She looked around desperately for a branch to hold out to Joni, and quickly found one lying on the ground. "Santiago, hang onto me while I hold this branch for Joni."

Santiago grabbed onto Leslie's legs as she lay down at the edge of the quicksand. Owen grabbed Santiago's legs. Working together, the three of them hauled Joni slowly out. It took a few tense minutes, but finally their leader was lying on firm ground.

Joni sat up. "LapTrap, how could you lead us into quicksand?" she accused him.

"I'm really, truly sorry," S.N.A.I.L.L. said. "My sensors just didn't pick up the difference in soil density. I'll try a lot harder to be careful."

"I hope so," said Joni, getting shakily to her feet. "That was *not* fun."

"Meantime, let's take a rest," said Owen. "I could really use some lunch right about now."

"Good idea," said Joni. "I sure hope Uncle Horace isn't too much farther."

"Not too, too much," said S.N.A.I.L.L.

Joni rummaged in her backpack and pulled out packages of gorp to distribute to everyone. They all munched on the nuts, seeds, and dried fruit, happy to be holding still for a few minutes.

"What on earth could have happened to Uncle Horace?" Joni mused.

"I can't imagine," said Santiago. "But he's pretty tough. He might be trapped somewhere, but I'll bet he's okay, wherever he is."

"He did get out of the clutches of that giant rutabaga somehow, I guess. The question is, where is he now?"

"I wish I could use my heartbeat detector," said Santiago, "but the sound of the bugs is just too overwhelming. It creates too much interference."

"Well, maybe LapTrap can lead us to him," said Joni.

"I sure hope so," said S.N.A.I.L.L. "But not if we don't get moving again."

"Okay, okay," said Joni.

"Hey, now *we're* starting to sound like LapTrap," said Owen with a laugh. "And LapTrap's starting to sound like us."

The hike through the jungle resumed, but it was no easier. First they were led through a rancid swamp, dripping with horrible-smelling green goo. And then it was the Valley of the Killer Hiccups.

Owen got them first. "Hey, guys, should we—*hic*—sing a song?" he proposed, as they walked through a long, misty valley.

"Maybe you should wait 'til your hiccups go away," said Santiago. "*Hic.*"

Joni laughed. "You guys both have the hiccups. That's so—*hic*—oh, no, I have them, too!"

The hiccups got stronger and more frequent, until the three of them were absolutely convulsed. Only Leslie seemed to be hiccup-free.

"Try drinking out of the other side of this," she said, offering Joni her collapsible cup filled with water from her canteen.

"O-*hic*-kay," said Joni. She leaned over and drank from the far side, which was usually a sure cure for hiccups, but it didn't happen this time. Santiago and Owen tried, too. Nothing.

"Boo!" yelled Leslie. She explained, "I'm inducing trepidation in you!"

Nothing. Joni, Owen, and Santiago were exhausted.

"We—*hic*—have to get—*hic*—out of here," said Joni. "Then maybe—*hic*—they'll go away."

"But which way do we go?" said Leslie.

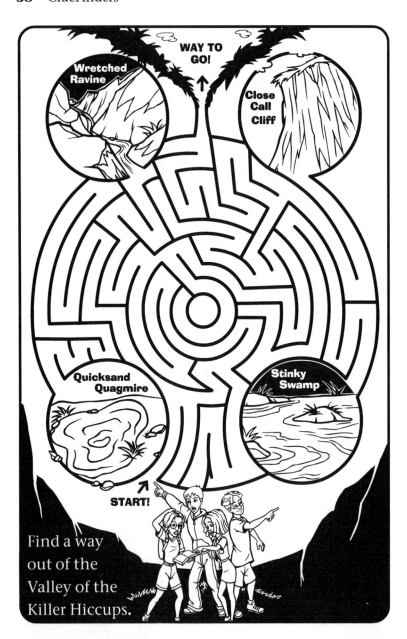

FOLLOW THAT BIRD

"I can get us out of here," said S.N.A.I.L.L. "Just follow me."

"I sure hope you can—*hic*—do it, LapTrap," said Joni. "Things haven't been going too well."

As they trudged along, hiccupping, they talked about hiccupping. "It's weird that Leslie doesn't have them, huh, dudes?" said Owen.

"Something must keep her from getting the hiccups," said Joni.

"I don't have natural immunity," Leslie said. "I'm not a person who doesn't *get* hiccups."

"And the bites," Joni reminded them. "When the rest of us have gotten covered with itching bites, Leslie hasn't."

"Most of the time, anyhow," said Leslie.

"Except for—*hic*—last night," said Joni. "The bugs left me alone last night."

"And then there's the poison whatever-plant," Owen added, scratching his leg. "Don't forget the poison whatsis, dudes."

"I got that," said Joni.

"I didn't," said Leslie.

"You lucked out," said Santiago.

As they kept walking through the jungle, Joni fell behind with Santiago. "Isn't it funny about LapTrap?" she whispered as the little computer bobbed ahead of them, out of earshot. "He seems so brave—just charging ahead, without worrying. I wonder what's gotten into him."

"And what's up with his forgetting all that important stuff?" said Santiago. "Like the cryptiles."

"How weird is that?" Joni agreed.

"Maybe his circuits just need a good cleaning," said Santiago.

"Maybe."

After about four more sweaty, itchy hours of tromping through the jungle, Joni put up one hand. "Everybody!" she said loudly. "Stop. Does this place look a little familiar to us?"

They looked around. "Oh, ye-e-a-ah," said Owen slowly. "I recognize that smelly orange flower over there. The one that reeks like old sneakers."

"And how about that big anthill up ahead?" said Santiago.

"We've definitely been here before," said Leslie.

"Twice," said Joni. "I had a hunch, so I started

keeping track."

"LapTrap!" they shouted. "You've been leading us in circles!"

"Would I do that?" he said in a hurt voice.

"Maybe not on purpose," Joni replied. "But that's exactly what you've been doing."

"He definitely needs his circuits cleaned," said Santiago, shaking his head. "As soon as we get back to San Francisco, I'm going to take him apart and give him a good going over."

The computer shuddered at the thought.

"I cannot believe this," said Joni. "Uncle Horace is in trouble! How much time have we wasted?"

"I think you're mistaken," said the fake LapTrap. "We're not going in circles. We'll be rescuing Uncle Horace any minute now. Honest!"

Joni made the time-out "T" sign with her hands. "Hang on, everybody. Maybe LapTrap needs his circuits cleaned and maybe he doesn't, but I think we'd better start thinking a little more clearly. Let's see what other kinds of information we can use."

"I have an idea that may just be constructive," said Leslie. She reached into her knapsack and pulled out a book. "This," she said, "is *The Flora and Fauna of Microsneezia,* by one Herman Berman. He was marooned here for a few weeks in 1913. I believe he had gone nuts from itching by the time he was rescued. Anyway, I found it in the library and brought it along just in case. It's pretty thin, because he wasn't here for long. But it just might have something that can help us."

"Well, it sure can't hurt to look at it," Joni said.

"What can you possibly learn from a book that you can't learn from me?" S.N.A.I.L.L. said in a snit. "It's probably full of wrong information. I've got state-of-the-art circuits."

"We can use both," said Joni firmly. "Leslie, see what you can find out."

Leslie sat down on a rock and began flipping through the book. "Uggh," she said, making a face. "It's no wonder Berman became unhinged. Giant slugs that smell like rotten fish. Biting bugs that like to live in the bottom of your sleeping bag... But how about this? Apparently there's a rare avian, found only on Microsneezia."

"Avian?" said Owen. "Is that a kind of bottled water?"

"Bird," said Joni.

"Anyhow, Berman dubbed this specimen the *birdhound*," Leslie went on. "He says it has the most acute sense of smell on earth. It can follow a trail for miles, and can smell things from huge distances."

"Let's see the picture," said Joni. "Maybe if we can find one of these birdhounds, it could somehow help us track down Uncle Horace."

"How?" asked Owen.

"Well," she said, reaching into her backpack, "I still have Uncle Horace's boot, the one that was dangling from the vine. I figured he'll probably need it when we find him. If we run across one of these birds, maybe we could let it smell the boot, just like a bloodhound, and it might lead us to Uncle Horace."

"Bizarre idea," said Santiago, "but it might just work."

They all gathered around Leslie's book to take a look at the picture. "Funny-looking critter, isn't it?" said Owen. "What else does the book say?"

"Well, let's see... it seems to be a lot like a dodo. It has very particular markings, and it can't fly."

"Anything else?" Joni asked.

"Aha," said Leslie. "It says the bird has a peculiar cry—like a Siamese cat, or a raccoon with a stomach ache."

"Oh, look, dudes," said Owen, reading over her shoulder, "the book has directions for making the sound. You put your hands this way, and then you stick two fingers in there, and then you sort of squeak like this…." He gave it a try, and out came a whiny, squeaky noise.

"If that's the right noise, it's a call only another birdhound could love," said Santiago. Within a moment, they heard rustling sounds near the jungle floor, coming from all directions. And then, surrounding them, the same strange-sounding squeaky call. It had worked! The birds were coming!

"Wow, Owen," said Joni. "Talk about getting results!"

Owen whispered, "Don't look now, dudes, but I think I see one of them near that bush."

"Hmm," said Joni. "It looks an awful lot like the picture. But is it the same bird? I can't be sure…."

"Look!" Santiago said quietly. "There's another. Is that one?"

"And there's another, over there!" said Joni. "It looks a little different, though!"

"They're all a little different from each other!" said Owen. "Which one is the real birdhound?"

Look closely. Which one is the real birdhound?

BREAKTHROUGH

"Hi, little guy," said Joni, bending down to talk to the birdhound. It really was kind of cute.

"Squonk," said the birdhound.

"So, do you think you could do us a little favor?" Joni asked respectfully. "If I gave you this boot to sniff, could you lead us to Uncle Horace?"

The bird stuck its whole head into Uncle Horace's boot. It sniffed deeply, for a long time. Then it pulled its head out of the boot and waddled off to the left.

"Follow that bird!" cried Joni.

"Don't follow that bird," said S.N.A.I.L.L. "Follow me!"

"Follow that bird!" said Joni. They took off after the bird.

None of them saw the anger and frustration on S.N.A.I.L.L.'s face.

◙▐◙

The birdhound, at least, did not lead them in circles. They were soon passing through scenery they had never seen before. And after a while, they found themselves breaking through the edge of the jungle, into a broad, grassy field of the most gorgeous yellow flowers they had ever seen.

"It's so wonderful to be able to see more than three feet in front of your face!" said Joni. They all plunged into the field. Bright yellow dust kicked up all around them as they stirred the flowers.

"Maybe this place isn't so bad after all," said Santiago.

"But… what is that incredible fetor?" said Leslie, sniffing the air.

"Forget the fetor," said Owen. "What's that horrible smell?"

"Uccch!" said Santiago. "It smells like a herd of angry skunks!"

Leslie was madly paging through her book as she walked, trying to figure out what the source of the stench was. "Stinkflowers!" she cried, pointing to a picture in the book. "That's what they are! Look, it's right here!"

They all gathered around to look at the book, holding their sleeves over their noses. Even the birdhound had its wing over its nose.

"'Prolonged exposure to the odor of the

stinkflower will produce loss of memory and even fits of howling,'" she read. "'Remove yourself from the area of the flower as quickly as possible, before irreversible damage sets in.'"

"Irreversible damage!" cried Owen. "Dudes! Let's get out of here!"

The birdhound seemed to be thinking the same thing, because it was waddling away as fast as its short little legs could carry it. They all held their breath and followed.

"Sure," said S.N.A.I.L.L., imitating LapTrap's usual put-upon tone. "Don't follow the computer. Follow the bird. The bird won't get you into trouble."

Near the edge of the field, Santiago began to look strange. He threw his head back. "Ow-woooo!" he howled. "Ow-ow-ow-woooooo!"

"Oh, no!" said Joni. "He's having a howling fit! We need to put something over his nose and mouth to act as a filter. Does anybody have anything?"

Owen searched his pockets. "Nothing," he said. "I could take off one of my socks, maybe."

"I have this," said Leslie, producing a blue bandanna.

"Perfect," said Joni. "Let's tie it around his face."

Working together, they positioned it over his nose and mouth. The howling subsided as they hurried out of the field. When they were beyond the field, they took off the bandanna.

He looked around at them in confusion. "Wha–what happened to me?" he said.

"Stinkflowers," said Joni. "Remind me not to plant any in my grandma's garden."

The birdhound looked back at them and struck off through the tall grass, looking determined. It seemed to be trying to say, "Follow me! This way!"

A few more minutes of wading through the long, blessedly sweet-smelling grass, and they suddenly stopped. They found themselves looking out over the edge of a huge, round depression, about fifty feet deep and a full mile in diameter.

"Wow," said Joni, speaking for all of them.

"What is that down there?" Owen asked, pointing to the bottom.

"It looks like a complex of cave entrances," said Leslie. "I wonder if anybody lives there."

Suddenly, with a *thwump,* something fell over the ClueFinders—a rope net.

"What the—" said Owen.

"You," said a voice. "Come with us."

They turned around. A strange group of people stood behind them. The strangers were covered with bug bites and itchy spots. Each one of them had a large box of tissues hanging from a vine around his or her neck.

"I guess you must all live here," said Joni, struggling against the netting.

"Can't you tell?" said the man who had spoken to them first. "We are the inhabitants of Microsneezia. I'm the mayor. And the president. You can call me Lou. Aah-*choo*."

"Bless you, Lou," said Joni.

"Thank you," he said, taking a tissue from his box and blowing his nose. Standing beside him was his wife. Her eyes were swollen from allergies and she had a big bug bite on her chin.

"It's kind of hard to live here, huh?" said Joni.

"You cannot imagine," he said. He slapped at a large bug. Then he zipped open his fanny pack, giving the ClueFinders a glimpse of what was inside: nose clips, bug spray, Calamine lotion, and dozens of other items to combat the effects of the island's awful environment. He squirted bug spray all over himself. "We all live in those caves down there to get away from the bugs. We spend our time watching travel videos, daydreaming about where we could move."

"Do you think you could take this net off us?" Joni asked. They were all enmeshed, except for S.N.A.I.L.L., who was hovering around.

"What do you think," the president asked the computer, "should we let them go? It's up to you."

"Nah. I think we should lock them up with the others," said S.N.A.I.L.L. in a much nastier voice than the ClueFinders had heard before.

The ClueFinders were beyond shocked. "LapTrap, how *could* you?" Leslie demanded.

A look of comprehension dawned on Joni's face. "He could," she said slowly, "because he's not really LapTrap. Are you?" she said, turning to the computer.

"Nope," said S.N.A.I.L.L. with a snicker. "Good thinkin', Lincoln. The name's S.N.A.I.L.L., at your service." He did a little dip, by way of a bow.

"That explains a lot," said Santiago. "What are you doing impersonating LapTrap?"

"No more questions," said S.N.A.I.L.L. "Take them away."

The ClueFinders were herded down a steep slope

toward the bottom of the basin. Ahead of them, the birdhound waddled in the same direction.

Finally, they all stopped at the mouth of one of the larger caves. A big rock was parked at its entrance, blocking it.

The birdhound went into a sort of point, like a hunting dog, with one leg bent and its nose pointing into the cave. Then it waddled off. It had done its job.

"Thanks, little dude," Owen said as the birdhound receded into the distance.

"I guess that about clinches it," said Joni. "Uncle Horace is definitely in there."

"And now you will be, too," said Lou. "Roll that rock away, everybody."

The townspeople worked together, grunting, to roll the huge rock away from the entrance. Then they shoved the ClueFinders into the cave, and rolled the boulder back into place behind them.

It was dark. Really dark.

There were dripping sounds all around.

"I... don't... like... this," said Santiago, trying not to sound too scared.

"I don't either," said Joni. "But we're just going to have to deal with it. We know Uncle Horace is in here. So we'll just have to feel our way along the walls until we find him."

"I hope LapTrap is in here with him," said Santiago. "I'm really worried about him."

"Let's keep talking to each other, just so we know we're all here," suggested Leslie.

"Even better, let's all hold onto each other," said Santiago.

With Joni in the lead, they started moving into the darkness, hanging onto each other's shirts.

"Maybe now is the time to admit to you guys that I have a thing about bats," said Leslie in a shaky voice.

"I have a thing about slime," said Owen.

"Spiders," said Joni.

"Rats," said Santiago with a shudder.

They continued in silence.

"Hey, look, you guys!" said Joni after a while. "There's a light up ahead!"

They all lurched to a stop, piling into each other. "Where?" said Owen.

"It's really faint," said Santiago. "It's just four little lines."

"Like the outline of a door!" said Leslie.

"Uncle Horace!" Joni cried. "Let's go,

ClueFinders!"

They inched their way forward as fast as they could, each one groping the walls with one hand and hanging onto a shirt with the other. Faintly, very faintly, they could hear a whiny voice from up ahead, behind the door. It was a familiar voice.

"Oh, sure, Dr. P.," said the voice. "I'll just run a computer model of the probabilities of all the substances known to the human race. No problem. And when I'm done, I'll fix you breakfast. Sure, don't hesitate to ask."

"LapTrap!" yelled all the ClueFinders happily. They inched a bit faster, and in a few moments they were banging on the thick metal door.

"Uncle Horace!" Joni shouted. "We're here to rescue you!"

The door opened immediately, and there was Uncle Horace, looking pleased and surprised. Inside the chamber was a small but decently equipped laboratory, complete with Bunsen burners, glass flasks, test tubes, and a centrifuge. "Glad you got my little message," he said to Joni.

"Loud and clear," she said, hugging him hard. "Are you okay? What have they done to you? Why are you stuck in here?"

He laughed. "One question at a time," he said. "I'm fine, first of all."

"Ask me if I'm fine," said LapTrap.

"Sorry. Are you fine, my brave little super-computer?" asked Joni.

"I'm all right I guess, thanks for asking," he replied. "As okay as I can be after having my circuits sizzled. It's a good thing they threw me in with Dr. P. here. He was able to fix me."

"Yeah, what is the deal on that creep S.N.A.I.L.L.?" Joni asked them.

"Rather a failed experiment, I'm afraid," said Uncle Horace. "The military put him together after LapTrap here turned out to be a bit—how shall I say it—understaffed in the courage department."

"Humph," said LapTrap.

"Sorry," said Uncle Horace. "At any rate, they wanted to make a machine with all LapTrap's wonderful computing skills, but more aggressive. Unfortunately, they made him *too* aggressive. He was basically insane, completely uncontrollable. When I convinced them to banish him instead of crushing him, I had no idea this was the island he'd end up on. When I arrived, I fell right into his lap."

"And then *LapTrap* fell into his lap," added Joni

with a laugh.

"So, what did S.N.A.I.L.L. do to get revenge on you?" Santiago asked.

"Well, as you know," said Uncle Horace, "this island is one big puddle of pestilence. The people who are stuck living here are absolutely bedeviled by it. S.N.A.I.L.L. was able to work his way into their confidence by promising that he'd use his brain power to help them solve their problems.

"Now, oddly," Uncle Horace went on, "I seem to be immune to the effects of these things. The bugs don't bite me, the flowers don't make me howl, I don't get the hiccups, none of it. I have no idea why. But S.N.A.I.L.L. had been lurking about, spying on me. When he noticed my immunities, he convinced Lou and the others to capture me, lock me up, and force me to work on figuring out what the source of the immunities was. They want it for themselves."

"The stinker," said Joni. "I knew something was weird about him."

"I do think the fault belongs to S.N.A.I.L.L.," said Uncle Horace. "Lou isn't bad. He's just desperate to find the secret of my immunity."

"That's so provocative," said Leslie. "By a

strange happenstance, I too have been largely immune."

Uncle Horace perked up. "Provocative indeed," he said. "Perhaps we share something—an item we wear, or eat, or even something in our genetic makeup—that protects us."

"I should add," said Leslie, "that I haven't been one hundred percent immune. Last night I was bitten repeatedly. But yesterday I wasn't at all, and this morning I was fine, too."

"And I was *only* immune last night," said Joni. "Didn't get bitten all night, and started again this morning. Weird, huh?"

"Hmm," said Uncle Horace. "I think it might be productive for us to compare everything we have been wearing, carrying, eating, drinking, or using. Maybe at the intersection of these things we'll find the source of the immunity."

"Let's make a chart," said Santiago.

"Great idea," agreed the team.

To make the chart, the ClueFinders and Uncle Horace had to lay out all their stuff, so they could compare and contrast. They emptied their pockets and backpacks onto the floor of the cave.

Leslie's eyes widened when Uncle Horace pulled

a piece of gum out of his pocket. "You have bubble gum?" she asked.

"Yes, I developed a fondness for it in Thailand," he said, a bit sheepishly.

"I like it, too," said Leslie.

"Look at that, dudes," said Owen. "Leslie and I both use the same exact lip balm."

Pretty soon, they had worked up a chart with all the information. Gazing at it, Joni said, "First, let's rule out all the things that Owen and Santiago had, because those two were never immune. But we have to look at all the things that Uncle Horace had, because he was immune all the time. And since Leslie and I were each immune some of the time, we have to think back to what we were doing, and what we were wearing, or eating, or holding. When we figure that out, we have to see what there is in common with Uncle Horace's stuff."

"Can you figure it out, dudes?" said Owen. "This is a mega-challenge."

Santiago	Joni	Leslie	Owen	Horace
knapsack	knapsack	knapsack	knapsack	knapsack
first aid kit	first aid kit	first aid kit	first aid kit	compass
sunscreen	sunscreen		sunscreen	notebook
sleeping bag	sleeping bag	sunscreen	sleeping bag	sleeping bag
video phone	gorp (carried)	sleeping bag	gorp (ate)	magnifier
gorp (ate)	Leslie's knapsack	book		bubble gum
heartbeat monitor		bubble gum	binoculars	

Identify one item that the people with immunities had when the bugs weren't bothering them.

CHAPTER 6

NOT OVER YET

Uncle Horace picked up the purple telephone on the counter. "The Microsneezians gave me this phone so I could call them when I have the answer," he said. "Now perhaps they'll let us out."

In ten minutes, the ClueFinders and Uncle Horace were standing outside the cave. The inhabitants of Microsneezia were gathered around them, beside themselves with excitement. Uncle Horace pulled out his piece of bubble gum.

"This," he announced, holding it up, "is the cure."

"Ooooh," said the crowd.

"Don't believe him!" called out S.N.A.I.L.L., hovering near Lou's shoulder. "He's trying to trick you." S.N.A.I.L.L.'s eyes narrowed. "He may poison you," he finished.

Joni waved at the nasty computer. "What does S.N.A.I.L.L. care if you find the secret to immunity?" she pointed out. "He's made of plastic and metal—nothing makes him sneeze. S.N.A.I.L.L. just wants you to keep Uncle Horace locked up forever, out of revenge."

Lou thought for a moment. Then he nodded at Uncle Horace. "Go ahead," he said. "We'll listen."

"It's your funeral," snarled S.N.A.I.L.L.

"Be quiet," said Lou. "I never trusted you anyway, you mean little so-and-so."

"Now," said Uncle Horace to Lou, "I'm going to give you a little piece, and we'll see what happens. It has to be very close to you to work. It'll probably work best if you chew it."

Uncle Horace gave Lou a tiny piece of bubble gum, and Lou started chewing energetically. Then everyone stood back and waited.

A gigantic mosquito came buzzing by, looking for someone juicy. It headed straight for Lou. Lou blew a small, defiant bubble at it. The bug stopped, then jumped straight up as if it had gotten an electric shock. It turned and buzzed away as fast as its wings could carry it.

"Amazing!" said Lou. Then he stopped rubbing his eyes. "My allergies!" he said. "My allergies are going away!"

He grabbed the bubble gum from Uncle Horace and turned to his wife. "Have some!" he said, breaking off a small piece. She popped it into her mouth. Lou stood back and watched.

"Your eyes!" he said. "You have green eyes! I've never seen them before!" Sure enough, the swelling was going down by the moment. "And your red bumps!" he said. "Look, they're gone!"

"I've stopped itching!" she said. "I haven't stopped itching ever—not in my whole life!"

They threw their arms around each other and began to dance in happiness. Leslie brought out most of her stash, leaving just a small amount for herself and her friends. The Microsneezians broke into a roar of joy, and everyone crowded around to get a piece of bubble gum.

"You'll be sorry!" sputtered S.N.A.I.L.L.

"No, I think it's you who's going to be sorry," said Lou. "Take him down to the cave and lock him in," he ordered his people. "Let him think about being a nicer computer. When he's ready to apologize he can come out."

"That'll be never!" spat S.N.A.I.L.L. as he was snared from the air and dragged off into the cave.

"Well, then," said Uncle Horace, "I think our job is done here. I forgive you for locking me up. And now my young friends and I will be taking our leave of you."

Lou and his wife exchanged looks. "I'm afraid we can't let you go," he said.

"Can't let us go? Why not?"

"This gum isn't going to last us for very long. I'm sorry to say that your job here is not over."

"You've got to be kidding," said Joni.

"Afraid not," said Lou. "You see, we can't let you out of here until you secure for us a perpetual supply of bubble gum."

"Where are we going to find that?" Santiago asked.

"In the bubble gum quarry, beyond the Whining Forest," said Leslie, whipping out her book. "According to *The Flora and Fauna of Microsneezia,* this island has the world's second-largest proven reserves of liquid bubble gum."

"That's right," said Lou. "But—"

"But, what?" Owen asked.

"No one has ever come back from beyond the dreaded Whining Forest alive," said Lou.

The ClueFinders all looked at each other. "Here we go again," said Joni.

Once again they slogged through the jungle, minus

Uncle Horace. The Microsneezians had decided to keep him as insurance that the ClueFinders would not simply take off.

"Didn't you think we were so done with this?" Owen said, chewing his small piece of gum vigorously. Now that they knew what the secret was, they were all chewing like crazy.

"If we're ever going to get off this island, we're going to have to do this last thing," said Joni.

"But this last thing is dangerous!" said LapTrap. "Why do you need to take me along anyhow?"

Joni smiled. "That's our LapTrap," she said, patting him on his lid.

"I just hope there really is a bubble gum quarry, dudes," said Owen. "If there isn't, we're in big trouble."

"According to Herman Berman there is," said Leslie. "But it's a pretty long hike from here. And before we get there, we have to go through this Whining Forest. I have no idea what *that* is. And then, right before the quarry, he has labeled something called Wordcliff."

"Whatever these things are," said Joni, "we have to get to this quarry, so we can go back, pick up Uncle Horace, and get out of here."

"At least he found his giant rutabaga, right?" said Owen. "That's something."

"It's not a giant rutabaga, it's a vegemecium," said Leslie. "I looked it up in the book."

"What's so special about it?" Santiago asked.

"The vegemecium is one enormous plant, with a root structure that probably travels all over this island," Leslie explained. "And it's all a single cell."

"Incredible," said Owen.

"Eeew, there's people here!" said a whiny voice.

"Of course there are people here," Joni said to LapTrap, looking annoyed. "Did Uncle Horace fix your circuits all the way?"

"I didn't say anything," said LapTrap.

"Then who did?" Leslie said, looking around.

"I did," said the voice. "So whaaat?"

"Hey, are you noticing what I'm noticing—that the forest looks different?" Santiago said.

"Oh, yeah, look at that," said Owen. "The trees are kind of farther apart. And taller."

"The Whining Forest!" said Leslie, snapping her fingers. "We must be there." The wind kicked up, and suddenly all the trees were whining.

"Tell them to go awayyy," whined one of them.

"It's not my turn, you do it," whined another.

"I don't *waant* to. Why do I have to?"

It seemed that the wind blowing through the trees caused them to whine. When the wind died down, so did the whining. When it got stronger, the whining did, too.

"I want someone to make them leave, right nowwww!" said a very tall tree near them.

"I can't do it, I'm tiiired," whined another.

Santiago put his hands over his ears. "I can't take this!" he yelled. "It's like being in a great big preschool before naptime! I'm losing my mind!"

Owen was so addled by the whining, he walked right into a tree and bonked his head.

"Heeyyy, watch ouuut," whined the tree.

"You watch out!" Owen retorted. "You're driving me crazy!"

"Okay, everybody," said Joni. "Here's what we're going to do. We're all going to stuff leaves in our ears to block the sound, and then we're going to walk out of this place as fast as we can. Otherwise we'll all go nuts."

"Good plan," said Owen, picking up a leaf. They all did the same, and soon they were marching at a good clip through the forest. The leaves did not block all the sound, however.

"They're not niiice."

"Why don't they leeeave?"

"I can't handle this any more!" said Leslie.

"Oh, no, you're sounding like them!" said Joni. "We better get out of here, and fast."

They picked up the pace, and in a few minutes, the landscape began to change again. It looked more like the old non-whining rainforest.

Finally, Joni took out her leaf earplugs. "I think the whining is behind us," she said.

"Thank heaven!" said Leslie.

Santiago was sniffing the air. "Do you guys smell what I smell? It's very faint, but—"

"Bubble gum!" shouted Leslie happily. "What a beautiful aroma! We're close, guys!"

As they continued toward the scent, it got stronger and stronger.

"You know what, guys?" said Joni. "I'm suddenly feeling a lot better. My last chew of bubble gum must have been fading, because my eyes were itching. But they're all better now."

"And the air is cleaner!" said Owen.

"And there are no bugs!" Santiago added.

They all breathed deeply, feeling the pestilence-fighting effects of the bubble gum quarry.

"Can you tell from your book how far it is?" Joni asked Leslie.

"Well, if we're going in the right direction, we should be at this place called Wordcliff soon," Leslie said, scrutinizing her book.

No sooner had she looked up from the pages than it was there in front of them: a sheer cliff face. It actually was a face, too. A craggy nose, eyes, and a mouth could be discerned in the bumps and fissures of the rock. The cliff completely blocked their path.

"So, here you are," said the face in a deep, booming voice. "What took you so long?"

The ClueFinders jumped about a foot each.

"Um… the Whining Forest?" said Joni. She shook her head. "I can't believe I'm talking to a rock."

"Shush," said the cliff. "Just follow directions, okay?"

"What directions?" Joni asked.

"The ones I'm about to give you, if you'll stop interrupting me. First, look for six hidden words. When you've found them, arrange the words into a sentence that makes sense. You can't get past me if you don't do it. Okey-doke?"

"Okey-doke," said Joni cautiously.

Sort the six hidden words into a sentence that tells the ClueFinders how to enter.

CHAPTER 7

LAP-TRAPPED!

"Okay," said Joni. "I think we've got it. 'Press the button under my nose.'"

"Look!" said Santiago. "There's a thing that could be a button, right there."

Joni approached the cliff and climbed up toward the nose, using stray vines and roots as footholds. "I'm almost—ugh—there," she grunted, stretching up to reach the button. She gave it a hard whack with the flat of her hand.

"Nice going," said the rock face, blasting her with the sound. "You're the first bunch that's been able to solve the puzzle. Have a nice day."

With that, a large door, previously invisible, suddenly opened in the rock. It made a grinding noise as it inched its heavy way open.

"Okay, ClueFinders, let's go!" said Joni.

They all ran for the door, and when they had all passed through, it ground shut again. Then, once more, they were in a dark passage.

"This is getting to be a habit," said Joni.

"A bad habit," said Owen.

Joni, who was first in line, felt her foot bang into something. "I think we've come to some stairs," she said, feeling around with her foot. "They go up." Carefully, she led them up the stairs.

"I just have one question," said Santiago. "Say we find this quarry. How are we going to get all that bubble gum back to the village?"

"We'll cross that bridge when we come to it," said Joni.

"Did I ever tell you guys," said LapTrap, his voice quaking, "that I have a thing about bats? And also spiders and slime and—"

Their laughter rang out in the dark.

"Hey, I think there's a door here," said Joni's voice. "I feel a doorknob. I'll try it and—WHOA!"

Light flooded in through a door. "Come out here!" Joni called. "But be careful!"

Slowly the others followed her out the door and into the brilliant sunlight. They found themselves on a high bluff. Below them, they saw what they had come so far to find: a vast quarry brim-full of pink goo. It was rotating rapidly, propelled by some huge underground sea of bubble gum.

"Dudes! Liquid crude bubble gum!" said Owen.

"When it air-dries it can be cut into pieces and

chewed," said Leslie, gazing at it rapturously.

"Be careful!" Joni warned her troops. "If you fall in, you'll get sucked under and drown."

"Bubble gummed to death!" said Santiago. "What a way to go."

"Joni," said Owen, "why don't you and I go down there and take a look around?"

"I'm game if you are," she said.

"See these long pink roots hanging over the edge of the bluff?" he said. "I think we can use them to climb down."

"Those are part of the root structure of the vegemecium," said Leslie.

"All the way over on this part of the island?" asked Santiago.

"According to the book, the roots are everywhere," Leslie explained. "They're just underground in most places."

"Well, they look pretty strong," said Owen. "I think they'll hold us."

"Okay," Joni said. "Let's go for it!" They high-fived, and then they each grabbed a dangling root and started down toward the quarry.

Suddenly, near the bottom, Owen's grip slipped. Joni gasped as he grabbed desperately for another handhold. But it was no use. He was falling.

Then, at the last moment, he hit a longer, thicker root that was sticking out of the side of the bluff below. He bounced off the root and shot upward, enabling Joni to grab him. He clung to Joni's root, breathing hard, as the other ClueFinders burst into applause.

"Hey, look! You guys, look!" said Santiago, pointing down. "The root!"

The bottom end of the root Owen had bounced off had been pushed down into the swirling pink glop. Now it was dangling into the bubble gum, drinking thirstily. And as it drank, it was changing. It was thickening, darkening in color, and sending out tendrils that shot down into the pool.

"The giant rutabaga loves the bubble gum!" said Joni. "Unbelievable."

"Do you know what this means?" said Leslie. "The bubble gum will be traveling all over the island through the plant. It's just possible that its beneficial effects will travel through it as well."

Now the other roots that hung over the quarry were sending out shoots of their own, which extended like bendy straws into the bubble gum. The vegemecium could not get enough of the stuff.

Suddenly the ClueFinders heard a deep rumble, and then a roar. "Landslide!" yelled Leslie. "Hang on, everybody!"

Leslie and Santiago held onto whatever they could up on the bluff, and Owen and Joni clung tightly to vegemecium roots. Rocks and debris tumbled into the quarry, some of them barely missing Owen and Joni. The roar continued for a few seconds, and then it stopped.

Behind the group on top, the structure of the cliff had partially collapsed.

"I think the face just rearranged itself," said Santiago.

"Uh-oh," said Leslie. "Where's our stairway?"

"Gone," said Santiago.

"How are we going to leave the way we came?" said LapTrap.

"I think we're not," said Leslie. "We're going to have to figure out some other way out of here."

"What's your book say?" Joni called up to her.

Leslie pulled the book out of her knapsack and searched the pages. "Nothing," she reported. "I don't think Berman ever got past the face."

"Then we'll have to figure it out for ourselves," Joni said.

Leslie and Santiago looked down for a while from their perch, thinking about it. Since the landslide, there were rocks sticking up here and there from the liquid, which had gone down considerably since the plant had started drinking it.

"You know," said Santiago finally, "I think it's just possible that we could—"

"Use the rocks to cross!" Leslie finished.

"Exactly!" said Santiago. "Like stepping stones."

"I think it could work!" Joni shouted up to them. "As long as we don't fall in. LapTrap, do you think you could do a quick photo scan of the rock patterns and figure out if it's possible to cross?"

"I guess I could," said LapTrap.

"There's a ledge down here that Owen and I can stand on for a while," Joni reported.

"Why don't we climb down to join them?" Santiago said. "That way we'll be ready to move out when LapTrap is finished."

"Good idea," said Leslie. The two of them chose roots to climb down while LapTrap hovered near them, taking photos and analyzing the data.

At last they were all clustered on the tiny ledge, hanging onto each other so nobody would fall off.

"How's it going, LapTrap?" Joni asked.

"I'm just about done," he said. "I've figured out the patterns and put the piles of rocks on a grid. Now I'm using X-ray imaging to analyze the stability of all the stones. When I'm done, I'll be able to tell you which ones to step on. You don't want to step on a shaky pile."

"We sure don't," Joni agreed.

In another few moments, LapTrap was done. "Okay," he said. "I've numbered the stones on the grid and printed it out for you. There's one good path across. You just have to step on the even-numbered ones to get across the quarry safely."

"Don't listen to him," said a familiar voice. "He's trying to sabotage us! You have to step on the *odd*-numbered stones, or you'll be in trouble."

They all looked up. Two identical yellow computers were hovering above them.

"LapTrap?" said Santiago.

"*S.N.A.I.L.L.?*" said Joni.

"Oh, no, S.N.A.I.L.L.'s gotten out somehow!" Owen concluded. "Which computer is which? How do we know who to listen to? If we listen to the wrong one, we'll be bubble gummed to death!"

Joni and Leslie exchanged intense looks. Then Joni nodded almost imperceptibly at Leslie.

"But if we listen to the right one," Leslie said casually, "it'll be as easy as strolling over to that great Mongolian restaurant on Clement Street."

"And," said Joni, "it's got to be easier than those camels we had to ride on the way here."

There was silence for a moment. Then one of the computers spoke.

"He-e-e-y," he said. "That restaurant's on California Street, not Clement. We've been there dozens of times."

"Right you are," said Joni with a grin. "Of course, S.N.A.I.L.L. doesn't know that."

"And," the computer continued, "you didn't ride camels to get here. You had donkeys."

S.N.A.I.L.L. sputtered and fizzled furiously as he realized that he'd been outsmarted.

The ClueFinders grinned. "What happened to your batteries?" Leslie asked, just to make sure.

"Your donkey tried to eat them," said LapTrap. "The nerve!"

"Helloo, LapTrap!" Joni cried. "Leslie, why don't you tie your bandanna around him so we can tell them apart?"

LapTrap coasted down to be festooned with a bandanna. "Looks delightful," Leslie said. "Maybe you could wear this all the time."

"Don't even think about it," said LapTrap over the sound of S.N.A.I.L.L.'s continued sputtering.

"Now," Joni asked LapTrap, "which rocks do we need to step on?"

"You want the odd-numbered ones," said LapTrap. "Don't go back once you've stepped on a stone. It might not be stable any more. And you won't be able to reach rocks that aren't next to you, in front of you, or diagonally ahead of you. The one who finds the path should lead the others across it. Okay?"

"Okay!" they all responded.

"Um—what should we do with *him*?" Santiago asked the group, pointing to S.N.A.I.L.L., who was zipping away over the quarry.

"Right now," said Joni, "we have to get out of here alive. Let's worry about him later. Does everybody have a printout of the grid?"

"Yes!" they all responded, holding up their copies.

"It looks as if one of us can swing out on a root to start with an odd-numbered one," Santiago said.

"Great!" said Joni. "Then, let's go! Odd numbers only! See you on the other side!"

Set a path for the ClueFinders to follow to this side, using only odd numbers. (No going backward!)

PORT TO PORT

Success! The whole team made it across without losing anyone. When it was over, they all sat on the opposite shore, catching their breath.

"Hey, look," Joni observed. "S.N.A.I.L.L.'s having trouble. He's still out there over the quarry."

"My batteries are running out," called S.N.A.I.L.L. weakly. His voice was slowed and deepened by lack of power. The ClueFinders could barely hear him. "I can't—make—it—across."

"Probably a ploy," said Leslie.

But it did not seem to be a trick, because S.N.A.I.L.L. was hovering lower and lower. "I'm faa-lling!" he said. With one last crackle, he plummeted downward.

"He must have used up all his battery power escaping from the cave," said Joni.

"What do we do?" said Leslie. "Save his execrable hide, or not?"

LapTrap sighed. "I can't let a fellow computer go down," he said. "It's against my nature. I'd better get out there and save him before he goes under."

"Can you do that?" Joni asked.

"I can do a port-to-port power jump," LapTrap replied.

"Isn't that dangerous?" said Santiago.

"I'm afraid so," said LapTrap gloomily. "My own power will dip momentarily, and I might not be able to stay up. But it's the only way." He zoomed off to save S.N.A.I.L.L.

"LapTrap! You're a hero!" said Leslie.

"Don't spread it around," said LapTrap. "I have a reputation to maintain."

It took him three attempts to shoot a cable directly into S.N.A.I.L.L.'s port. At last the port-to-port connection was established.

"Zzzzt!" went the power from LapTrap to S.N.A.I.L.L.

S.N.A.I.L.L. crackled to life, soaring up out of the swirling gum as LapTrap went into a momentary swoon and dipped perilously close to the surface of the liquid. But soon they were both heading to the shore, still connected.

"You are one lucky laptop," Joni said to S.N.A.I.L.L. when they were safely over the land. "A lot of computers would have let you drown."

"I think we'd better tie a rope to him before

LapTrap disconnects," said Santiago. "That way we can keep an eye on him."

Owen pulled a rope from his knapsack and tied it securely around S.N.A.I.L.L. "We can fly him like a kite," he said with a grin.

"Grrr," said S.N.A.I.L.L., still weak.

◙▯◙

The trip back to the village was not too difficult, as it turned out. All they had to do was follow the sound of the Whining Forest. This time, they stuffed leaves into their ears *before* entering.

After that, they knew the way. "Hey, do you guys notice what I'm noticing?" Joni said. "Everything smells better."

"And the bugs!" said Santiago. "They're gone!"

"Whoa, you're totally right, dudes!" said Owen.

"I think it worked," said Leslie. "The plant has absorbed the bubble gum through its root system, and distributed it everywhere on the island. And now it's transpiring the bubble gum molecules everywhere, thereby getting rid of all the bugs and obnoxious smells."

"Transpiring?" said Owen.

"Breathing," Leslie replied.

"A happy ending," said Joni.

At last, many hours later, they stumbled into the village. When the villagers saw the ClueFinders team approaching, they broke out into cheers and shouts. "You saved our island!" said Lou. "Hooray!"

"You did sort of make us," said Owen crankily.

"I guess we did," said Lou, hanging his head.

"And now you have to turn over Uncle Horace," said Joni. "Right this second."

"No problem," said Lou.

Uncle Horace strolled out of one of the caves, sipping on a pink drink with a little umbrella in it.

"Thank goodness you're okay!" said Joni.

"I'm fine," said Uncle Horace. "I knew the ClueFinders would succeed." He gave Joni a hug.

"Hey, guys, take a look at S.N.A.I.L.L.," said Santiago. The computer was lying on the ground in a state of collapse. They shook their heads.

"It's hard to feel like helping him out," said Joni.

"It's not his fault he is the way he is," said Uncle Horace. "He was made that way. It's just that miserable devil chip they put into him."

"Could you extract it while he's out of commission?" Leslie asked.

"Hmm. I suppose I could. Good idea," Uncle

Horace said. "And then LapTrap can give him another power boost to get him going again."

"I ought to give him a whack on the serial port for having us all locked up," said LapTrap.

Everyone laughed—even Lou.

"You can use your old lab to work on him," said Lou's wife.

Uncle Horace and LapTrap both shuddered. "Only if you give us a flashlight this time," said Uncle Horace.

Uncle Horace picked up the inert S.N.A.I.L.L., and he and LapTrap disappeared into the cave.

"I sure hope he's nicer when he comes out," said Owen. "He was one mean little computer."

"Uncle Horace can do it, if anyone can," said Joni.

In about twenty minutes they reappeared. S.N.A.I.L.L. now had a racy blue stripe painted on him so everyone could distinguish him from LapTrap, and he was buffed to a brilliant shine.

"Wow, he looks really spiffy," said Joni.

"Gosh, thanks!" glowed S.N.A.I.L.L. "Do you really think so?"

"Definitely, dude," said Owen.

"Gee whiz, you guys are the best!" said

S.N.A.I.L.L.

"So," Joni said to Uncle Horace with a smile, "I guess you took that chip out, huh?"

"It was easy as pie," said Uncle Horace. "Now he'll be friendly, cheerful, loyal, and brave."

"Especially cheerful!" said S.N.A.I.L.L.

"Sort of annoyingly cheerful, if you ask me," Joni whispered to Leslie behind her hand.

"This is great," said Lou. "Now S.N.A.I.L.L. can help us with our big new plans for the island. Now that it's a bug-free paradise, we can make it into a major resort. And we're thinking about renaming Inner Microsneezia," he went on. "We're probably going to call it Ultra-Marvelosa."

"Terrific idea," said Joni impatiently. "Can we go now?"

After a good deal of hunting, they found the bug-damaged balloon. It was crumpled in the far corner of the stinkflower field, which now smelled wonderful.

"Let's get this thing fixed up and ready to roll, ClueFinders!" said Joni. And like the great team that they were, they set to work patching the holes, repairing the burner, and fixing the basket, until the whole thing was good as new.

Everyone from Microsneezia gathered around. "Come back soon!" said Lou as they lifted off.

"Not that likely," Owen called down. "Have a great life, though!"

"Have a really fabulous flight!" S.N.A.I.L.L. called, blinking his lights at them.

They rose quickly into the air. "It's fortunate that the propane tanks weren't damaged," Uncle Horace said as they waved goodbye to the crowd.

"I'm glad you brought up the subject of propane tanks," said Santiago. "Because I'm looking at the gauge right now, and it says we have about nine hours' worth of gas left."

"LapTrap, how fast is the wind blowing?" Joni asked.

LapTrap stuck out his wind velocity sensor. "23 miles per hour," he said.

"We have to figure out whether we can get someplace on the fuel we have left," said Joni. "What if we run out in the middle of the ocean?"

"Someplace or other, here we come!" said Owen. "We hope."

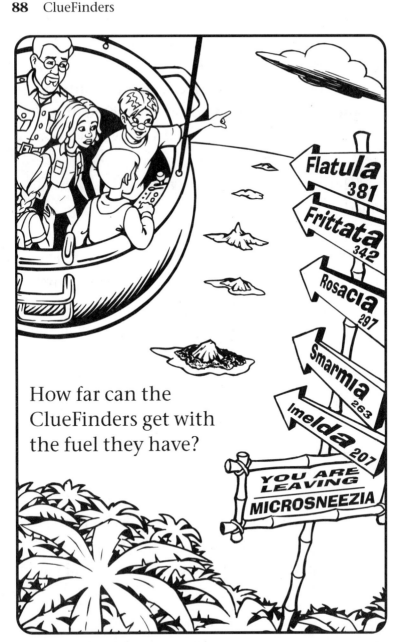

How far can the ClueFinders get with the fuel they have?

EPILOGUE

The journey home was not easy, but they made it. This time, they actually did have to ride camels on part of the trip.

Uncle Horace was thrilled to be home to tell the world about the vegemecium. A couple of months after their return, his article about the discovery was published to great acclaim in the scientific journal *Odd One-Celled Plants with Pink Roots*.

Joni tried out Santiago's gift. It didn't work very well as a reticulating transponder, but it made a great soap dispenser. Owen borrowed his skateboarding book from Joni and forgot to give it back, which was okay with Joni. Leslie made a study of how the Sanskrit language influenced English.

The only one who seemed a little bit the worse for wear was LapTrap. It took him months to stop jumping every time he caught a surprise glimpse of himself in a storefront window or mirror.

Psst! These are the answers to the puzzles that are at the end of each chapter.

Chapter 1
HELP
TRAPPED
33 S LAT
97 W LONG

Chapter 2
HEAD NORTH BY NORTHEAST

Chapter 3

START!

Chapter 4
The birdhound on the far left is the correct one.

Chapter 5
It's the bubble gum!

Chapter 6
Press the button under my nose to enter.

Chapter 7
Stones 7, 13, 11, 97, 65, 33, 5, 9, 17, 51, 55, 71, 75, 17, 301 are the path.

Chapter 8
Imelda